LILA PRAP

DRAGONS?!

What are these DRAGONS?

FIREFLY BOOKS

Our mom is always finding strange books. The last one said we are descended from dinosaurs.

As a descendant of dinosaurs you seem to hatch even weirder creatures!

Who would have thought that we have cousins that can bite elephants!

MEANT: A BIG SNAKE.

★ In ancient times, travellers claimed they saw dragons, strange, snake-like creatures, living in remote corners of the world. More than 2000 years ago, a Roman scholar named Pliny the Elder was the first person to write an encyclopedia about all different kinds of animals, even dragons. Later, imaginative people who wrote about dragons added different body parts to the snake-like dragon including wings, legs and strange heads.

Why did they add various body parts to snakes?

Pliny the Elder said the biggest dragons live in India. When the weather was hot, they attacked elephants and drank elephant blood to quench their thirst. The dragons hid in the trees. When an elephant walked under the tree, the dragon jumped down and wrapped itself around the elephant's legs. The dragon sank its sharp teeth into the elephant and sucked out all its blood unless the elephant could fall on top of the dragon and squash it.

This one is like a chicken, wearing a mask of a raging bull!

If someone makes me angry, I look horrifying, too.

This "big snake" has a few extra parts added!

LOOK HORRIFYING!

★ Thousands of years ago people told stories about dragons that were the gods that had created the world and ruled people's lives. In Mesopotamia, there is a story called *Enuma Elish* about dragons written on clay tablets 3500 years ago. The story tells how Tiamat, a huge snake that ruled the oceans, and Apzu, the god of fresh water, married and had many children, all of them young gods.

So, did these weird creatures lay eggs?

Tiamat was a caring mother but had children that were real horrors. Abzu, her husband, was so angry at the children that he wanted to kill them. But the children killed him first. Tiamat was furious and created an army of dragons and monsters to help her finish off her children. In the battle, her grandson, Marduk, killed her. He created heaven and earth from her body and created people from the blood of her husband's body.

Well, that is ridiculous. It looks like anyone with a little time can lay eggs.

They had quite unusual nests, it seems!

If you're laid in a nest like that, the first thing you would do is poop yourself from fear!

CHICKENS!

★ Thousands of years ago, the Ancient Greeks met travellers from the East who told stories of monsters called Griffons. These beasts had big, hooked beaks and were guardians of gold. Herodotus, a Greek historian, wrote: "In the mountains of the north are the largest troves of gold. It is said that a one-eyed people, the Arimaspi, steal the gold from the griffons." People believed that griffons laid their eggs in nests full of gold nuggets.

So, did the dragons collect gold like crows do?

Pictures of griffons are found in both Egyptian and Mesopotamian art but the Greeks first carried the stories of griffons to Europe. Some writers thought the griffons were dragons. Other writers said a griffon's body was eight times larger than a lion's body and that a griffon was 100 times stronger than an eagle. Griffons were said to have talons larger than an oxen's horns and so strong they could grab a horse and rider and carry them to the griffon's nest.

I'm also guarding a treasure! The eggs that my children will hatch from.

You guard them carefully! So that dragons don't hatch from them!

Our mom doesn't lay dragons, dad!

GUARDED TREASURE!

In an ancient Greek story the brave Argonauts accompanied Jason to the island of Colchis to get the Golden Fleece. But the fleece was protected by a dragon that never slept. Jason would not have succeeded in stealing the Golden Fleece from the dragon if he hadn't been helped by the king's daughter, Medea, who used her magic to put the dragon to sleep. Medea was no ordinary witch. She had a carriage that was pulled by two dragons!

So dragons worked for people, instead of dogs or horses?

The king had promised to give the Golden Fleece to Jason if, using two bulls that had bronze legs and breathed fire, he plowed a field and sowed dragon's teeth in the furrows.

Then, when soldiers grew from the teeth, Jason would have to defeat them in battle. Jason fulfilled the task with Medea's help but, instead of giving Jason the Golden Fleece,

the king attacked him. Jason and the Argonauts fled along with Medea and the stolen Golden Fleece.

How can we be related to pesky monsters? We're the nicest creatures in the world!

I know one pesky monster! Your mother, my dear!

Our granny isn't a pesky monster! You can be even more pesky than her, dad!

E JUST PESKY MONSTERS!

After stealing the Golden Fleece, the Argonauts were chased by the king's army. They first fled along the River Danube, then along the River Sava and stopped in the marshes near Ljubljana. There they took their ship apart and used the wood to build houses for the winter. But a fire-vomiting dragon flew over from the marsh and burned down some of the houses. The dragon grabbed one of the Argonauts with its claws and flew back to its den.

Dragons vomited fire? Wow!

Jason and Medea set off in pursuit of the dragon. They found it on an island in the middle of the marsh. Medea put the dragon to sleep and then Jason wrapped a chain around its snout and blocked its nose. When the dragon woke up, it wanted to breathe fire, but the fire ended up in its stomach. The dragon exploded and the Argonauts were able to spend the winter there in peace, and in spring re-assembled the ship. In memory of this, Ljubljana has a dragon in its coat of arms.

SOME DRAGONS VOMITED

Why?

Firefighters used so much water to put out a dragon that was vomiting fire, that for a long time afterwards, the dragon vomited water.

When I was sick, I also vomited something resembling water. Does that mean I'm a dragon?

WATER!

Some people blamed dragons for the unusual bursts of water that came out of the ground near the spot where Jason defeated the marsh dragon. The water burst out twice a day, always at the same time. What was even more unusual, the water would also gush out if you screamed and poked at the hole with a stick. Together with the water, strange animals came out. People thought these strange animals were baby dragons.

So, are dragons real or not?

A local story said that a dragon lived in the cave was the source of the water. Because the dragon was too big to come out of the hole, twice a day it pushed out extra water from the cave. But if it was teased, the dragon threw the foamy white water out with such force that some of its babies came out with the water. The Slovene scholar Valvasor found that the babies were actually a species of salamander, also known as the human fish.

For a long time people believed that dragons were real, but now they don't.

Now, people believe in all sorts of silly things, but not in dragons, it seems.

I hope there really are no dragons. I won't be able to sleep if I see monsters like that.

★ Until a couple of hundred years ago even scientists assumed that unusual old skeletons they found belonged to dragons and wrote about them as if they had been real creatures. When a large skull was found in Europe, it was proudly declared to be a dragon's skull and exhibited in a museum. The skull even served as a model for a statue of a dragon. Later scientists found that the skull actually belongs to a rhinoceros from before the Ice Age.

Good job they didn't find a number of heads! What a monster that would be!

In a marsh near Klagenfurt a dragon attacked livestock and travellers who wanted to cross the nearby river. In order to kill the dragon, a Carinthian duke built a tower next to the marsh and used an ox, wrapped in a chain covered with hooks, as a bait for the dragon. The dragon tried to eat the ox, got caught on a hook like a fish and was killed. The town of Klagenfurt still has a dragon standing in front of a tower on its coat of arms.

Was one head not enough for the silly things they did?

If I had more than one head, I could crow in a trio or a quartet. That would be great!

If they had a number of heads, they must have spent the whole day brushing their teeth.

THAN ONE HEAD!

In some stories, dragons have three, seven, nine or even a hundred heads. Killing a dragon with many heads was almost impossible. If you didn't chop off all its heads at once, new ones would immediately grow back. An evil dragon, Gorynych, had many heads and lived in the mountains of south-eastern Russia. An unusual statue to commemorate this dragon was built and, so the story goes, every now and then fire bursts out of all its heads.

People really are funny! They put evil dragons on the town coat of arms or erect statues to them!

The dragon Gorynych was a great danger to everyone living in the valley next to the mountain where it had his den. One day, a heroic young man called Dobrynya tricked the dragon and was going to kill it. To save its life the dragon promised Dobrynya that it wouldn't bother people anymore and Dobrynya let it go. But the dragon soon kidnapped the prince's daughter. In a fight lasting three days, Dobrynya killed the dragon and saved the princess.

If dragons really are real, we should make a dragon statue as soon as possible!

While I'm in charge of defending this henhouse, you don't need any statues!

We'll make a statue of you, dad, if a dragon attacks while you're asleep!

WITH DRAGON STATUES!

The Vikings, bold seafarers, had many dealings with dragons. Vikings called their stories sagas. One saga describes Kraken, a sea monster feared by all sailors. The Kraken was so big that when its head was sticking out of the sea, many travellers mistook it for an island. But when the dragon opened its huge mouth it gobbled up the crew together with the ship. In order to scare away such monsters, the Vikings put a statue of a dragon on the prow of their ships.

The dragons probably weren't the only ones scared away!

Other seafarers also saw horrifying dragons while sailing the seas. They described them so convincingly that many scholars included dragons in their scientific books. Dragons were even drawn on old naval maps, together with the following warning: *Here be Dragons!* Now it is assumed that the sailors saw large octopuses or whales and described them as dragons.

These two are looking at each other like the dogs Max and King next door!

That's nothing compared to the looks the rooster next door and I exchange!

Good job you only look at each other!

Since dragons were magnificent beings, some military units depicted them on their emblem. At the head of the Roman army there was always a soldier carrying a dragon puppet on a stick. When the Romans conquered Wales the Welsh took the image of a dragon as a symbol for their own army. The red dragon on the Welsh flag commemorates their victory over the Saxons, who used a white dragon on their flag.

So the dragons were used to depict winners?

One day, the deathly screams of a red dragon could be heard all around Wales. The red dragon was fighting the white dragon. In order to end the dragons' battle, the British king dug a hole in the middle of England and filled it with mead. During their fight, the dragons fell into the hole, got drunk on the mead and fell asleep. The king then put them in jail. Centuries later they were freed and the red dragon finally defeated the white intruder.

This one looks more like a furious lady bird!

I think I'm the most horrifying dragon anywhere!

Even <u>we</u> aren't afraid of dragons that look like angry lady birds!

TO DEPICT LOSERS!

★ When ancient European peoples believed there were different gods that looked after the harvest, the people and the planets in the sky, dragons usually represented the untameable forces in nature. When people came to believe in a single god who watches over everything, the ancient gods were forgotten and dragons came to represent evil. To overcome evil, various brave men fought with dragons and killed them wherever they found them.

This means that dragons' days are over in Europe!

St Martha fought with a dragon in France and saved the townspeople of Nerluc who had been intimidated by the dragon for many years. As the monster was about to eat someone walking past St Martha showed it a cross made from two branches and the dragon tamely followed her to the town, where it was killed. Since then, the town has been called Tarascon. There is a statue of the dragon in the town and every year a parade is held in honor of St Martha.

What's this? A snake with a plume?

The plume on my tail is a hundred times more magnificent! So why haven't I been chosen as a god?

You are a god, dad! You're always saying that the sun only rises if you crow!

AROUND THE WORLD!

The Aztecs believed in dragons that resembled large snakes with wings, feathers or horns. The dragons were worshipped as gods who had created the world and were masters of nature and life. Large temples were built where plants, animals and even people were sacrificed to the gods. Some of the temples were astronomical observatories. When Europeans arrived, bad times came for both the dragons and the people.

So, the dragons were finished everywhere!

Among the most important Aztec deities was Quetzalcoatl, the Feathered Serpent. According to one story, after catastrophes had for the fourth time destroyed the world, Quetzalcoatl went underground and by splashing its blood on the bones of dead people, returned them to life. He supplied corn to the people to keep them from starving. Because he sacrificed his blood to bring people to life, the Aztecs sacrificed human blood in gratitude.

Finally, relatives we don't have to be embarrassed about!

Relatives are nothing but trouble! Has anyone from Asia ever sent me anything?

You haven't sent anything to anyone either, dad!

ARE STILL WORSHIPPED!

★ Unlike other dragons, East Asian dragons are usually friendly and sensible. They only cause trouble if someone makes them really angry. In ancient China, dragons were worshiped as gods that controlled the water and weather and were a symbol of strength and happiness. Chinese emperors considered themselves to be descended from dragons. Once a year, festivities honor the dragons and every twelfth year is called the "Year of the Dragon."

Nice! But I still don't know why dragons should be the descendants of chickens!

Chinese dragons resemble snakes that have four legs, a horse's head and deer antlers. They can change shape and size to whatever they want and, although they don't have wings, they can fly. Most often, dragons are depicted playing with a pearl, which signifies wisdom, eternal life, strength and the moon. There are four royal dragons which rule the seas and a magnificent yellow dragon which represents the origin of the universe.

So, hens produce chicks and roosters strange monsters?

Don't be silly. I don't lay eggs. It's science fiction!

I'm very lucky not to have hatched from a rooster's egg. I'd look a little strange!

ROOSTER EGGS!

Pliny the Elder described a small snake that had a mark in the shape of a crown on its head. The basilisk, as he called the creature, did not move like other snakes but had the front part of its body raised. It was very poisonous and even a look from it was fatal. Its only enemy was the weasel. The basilisk excited people's imagination for centuries, scholars added parts to it and artists tried to depict it as scarily as possible.

By adding eight chicken thighs and a rooster's head to it?

Because of the crown on its head, scholars called it the "little king." Some wrote that the basilisk hatched from the egg of a snake or a toad that had been kept warm by a rooster. Others thought the basilisk came from the egg of a seven-year old rooster that had been laid at midnight at the time of a full moon on a heap of manure and had been kept warm by a snake or a toad. The Bible says that all dragons are descended from the basilisk.

Roosters hatch from hen eggs, and dragons from rooster eggs. So we really are the parents of dragons!

It's me who produces dragons, not you!

Dad, don't "father" any dragons. We don't want stepbrothers and sisters like that!

★ People kept adding parts of other animals to the image of the basilisk for so long and ascribed so many horrible characteristics to it, that with time it turned into the most horrific dragon we can imagine – the rooster dragon. Like the basilisk, it kills with its eyes. It sets grass and bushes on fire and breaks stones on its way. It can kill with its breath, its touch or even by just touching an object that someone possesses. It can only be destroyed by a rooster or a weasel. The rooster's crowing is deadly to it.

I have to learn to crow as soon as possible!

Some people were convinced that the rooster dragon hatched from the egg of a rooster kept warm by a snake or a toad. Others claimed that this kind of dragon was hatched from an egg of a basilisk kept warm by a rooster. For protection, people used to travel with a mirror or a rooster in their pocket. On hearing the sound of a rooster the dragon was struck by terrible pains and died. If the monster sees itself in a mirror it also dies.

A FIREFLY BOOK

This edition published in English 2019 by Firefly Books Ltd.
Copyright © Mladinska Knjiga Zalozba 2019
Translation © Lila Prapp and Mladinska Knjiga Zalozba
First published in Slovenia 2019 under the title Zmaji?! By Lila Prap

First printing, 2019

Library of Congress Control Number: 2019937170

Library and Archives Canada Cataloguing in Publication
Title: Dragons?! / Lila Prap.
Other titles: Zmaji. English
Names: Prap, Lila, 1955- author.
Description: Translation of: Zmaji?!
Identifiers: Canadiana 20190087404 | ISBN 9780228102076 (hardcover)
Subjects: LCSH: Dragons—Juvenile literature.
Classification: LCC GR830.D7 P7313 2019 | DDC j398.24/54—dc23"

Published in Canada by
Firefly Books Ltd.
50 Staples Avenue, Unit 1
Richmond Hill, Ontario
L4B 0A7

Published in the United States by
Firefly Books (U.S.) Inc.
P.O. Box 1338, Ellicott Station
Buffalo, New York
14205

Printed in China

Here, chick chick chick chick chick! ...

Maybe dad's trying to say she's some sort of dragon. She provides us with corn grains, and often takes away a kind of sacrifice — an egg or a hen!

You and your conspiracy theories! Rose brings us grain because she likes us.

I'm really interested
in what kind of dragon
he could make. But we
don't have any toads
or snakes!

I'm afraid dad
will really try to
hatch a dragon!

Maybe we can ask
our dog or cat to
warm his eggs?